Jeanne Willis has written over seventy books, including poetry and novels, and has won several prestigious children's book awards. She lives in north London with her family of creatures that features two children, a couple of cats and some pet rats.

One day, on a trip to the zoo, Jeanne struck up a conversation with a retired gorilla keeper. He explained how he was able to translate a gorilla's body language, but that no one else understood her . . . It made Jeanne wonder: if that gorilla could communicate verbally, what would this supposedly 'dumb' creature have to say?

Praise for *Dumb Creatures*

'This short novel is simply but compellingly written and utterly believable, a lovely book about the power of trust and the importance of not underestimating those we cannot always understand' *Observer*

Also by Jeanne Willis

Rat Heaven

DUMB CREATURES

JEANNE WILLIS

ILLUSTRATED BY NICOLA SLATER

MACMILLAN CHILDREN'S BOOKS

First published 2004 by Macmillan Children's Books

This edition published 2005 by Macmillan Children's Books
a division of Macmillan Publishers Limited
20 New Wharf Road, London N1 9RR
Basingstoke and Oxford
www.panmacmillan.com

Associated companies throughout the world

ISBN 0 330 41804 1

1 3 5 7 9 8 6 4 2

A CIP catalogue record for this book is available from
the British Library.

Printed and bound in Great Britain by Mackays of Chatham plc, Kent

For the children of Hazelwood Junior School

And with special thanks to Tom Orsler

I can hear. I can think. I just can't talk. Nobody knows why. Just because I can't talk doesn't mean I have nothing to say. I have a lot to say, but, if I try to speak, it sounds like a dog bark. Or a cat yowl. Or a rat squeak.

People laugh and call me stupid. They must think I'm deaf or why would they be so unkind? Maybe they think that if I can't speak, I have no feelings. But I do.

If people would only shut up and watch, they could see that I have feelings. They would read it in my eyes. See it scribbled on my face. They could tell by the way I hold my body. Only they never keep still enough. They never keep quiet enough to notice.

I use big gestures because I have big feelings, all bottled up. I thought if I used big enough gestures, everyone would know what I was trying to say. Sometimes a thick gush of words comes up from my stomach into my mouth. It stings the back of my throat, but it won't come out. I choke everything back down.

I'm eleven now. I go to an ordinary junior school. I use sign language. I can sign to my parents and to Ruth, my speech therapist – but I can't hold a proper conversation with the people in my class. They talk to me, but only in the way they might talk to an animal they were fond of.

'Play ball, Tom?'

They ask questions, but they always answer them for me.

'You like football, don't you, Tom?'

No, I don't like football. I just kick the ball around in the playground because everyone else does. If I stand behind the white line to watch the game, the girls mother me. They treat me like a baby. I wish they wouldn't. I wish they would look at me the way they look at the other boys. I watch them looking at Ryan and Jamie and Matt. I see their eyes sparkle. They sway their shoulders. They blush.

They never do that to me. They play families with me. I'm always the baby or the dog. Never the father. They're only trying to be kind, but inside I want to scream. Sometimes the scream slips out and the girls run off giggling. I make them nervous. They think I'm a poor little mad boy. I'm not. I'm as intelligent as anybody. I just can't talk. I feel like a foreigner in my own country sometimes.

I can never have a private conversation. Sign language is silent, but everyone can see it. People might not understand what's being said, but, then again, they might. It's impossible to tell. I don't want everyone knowing my business, but what if I need to ask something very personal? About growing up, perhaps. I can't whisper it in sign language. The only people I can ask are my parents. Only there are some things no one wants to discuss with their mum and dad. There are things boys only want to talk about with other boys. I have no boys to talk to. None of the boys at school can sign. I have to get all my answers from books.

It's hard to share anything more than the simplest thought when you can't speak and people can't sign. That's why they think I'm simple. But I'm not. I have very deep thoughts. Beautiful thoughts. Once, when I was on a school trip, I saw a hawk hovering above a meadow. Its wing tips fluttered like tissue. It was watching. Waiting. No one else had seen it. I thought if the rest of the class could just see that hawk, it would make their day. They would see how magical something so silent could be. I pulled at the teacher's jacket and pointed at the sky.

'What, Tom? Aeroplane?'

I shook my head. Without warning, the hawk shot like an arrow into the long grass. I saw it rise with a snake twisting in its talons. It was brutal. Magnificent. It took my breath away. I pointed into the sky again. I jumped up and down and pointed.

'All right, Tom . . . Tom saw an aeroplane, everybody.'

The teacher patted my shoulder. She didn't even look up. No one bothered to look up. They were too busy talking. Yak, yak, yak. My hawk melted against the sun. Invisible dream bird. We all had to draw what we saw on the field trip. I drew the hawk. It was a good drawing.

'Just like a hawk,' the teacher said, 'only we

didn't see a hawk.'

I did. I saw the hawk. I see things that people who talk will never see. If only they knew what they were missing, sinking in their sea of noise. Talk drowns truth, I swear.

I go to the zoo to be with creatures that can't speak. I go to the aquarium and watch the turtle swimming in silence. She is too big for the tank. That is what she is saying with every part of herself. The bubbles that pour from her nose are speech bubbles in a cartoon, in a comic: 'I am too big for my tank. Why does this tiny ocean have glass sides? Where can I stop and lay my eggs?'

Am I the only one who understands? Worse, do people who can speak actually understand but ignore what they are being told? That is what I am afraid of.

The zoo isn't far from my house. Down the high street and up a hill. I am allowed to go there by myself now. Now my mother is pregnant. People say it's good that she is expecting another baby. They say that, then they see me watching and stop in the middle of the sentence. I know how the sentence ends though. It ends like this: 'This baby will be normal. You will have someone to talk to.'

She has my father to talk to. She has the whole world to talk to. I have no one. I need no one. I go to the zoo to be with creatures that want to tell me things. Creatures in a foreign land. Aliens from another planet. Camel next to wolf. Tiger next to penguin. Bear next to giraffe. What could they possibly have in common to talk about? You would be surprised.

I am a Friend of the Zoo. I have paid my membership. I have twelve free tickets to visit whenever I please. I stand for hours in front of each cage. I want to get to know each animal for himself. For herself. I watch and listen. They watch and listen too.

Sometimes, I touch. I have touched the rhinoceros. I know why she wrinkles up her tiny eyes and snorts. She has told me many things.

She told me in the way she pawed the sand in the moat and rubbed her horn against the concrete wall and groaned. She smelt of Africa.

I looked into the tiger's eye – it was as green as a mangrove and as deep. In the pools of its eye, I saw a flame. It was as weak as a candle on a cake. It flickered and faltered but it would not go out. If I dared to blow in the tiger's eye, I could have snuffed it out, but something always kept it burning. The hot breath of India. When the tiger died, he would be the saint of tigers. They would hang garlands round his neck and respect him.

One day, my mother said she wanted to come to the zoo with me. She needed to get out of the house. Did I mind?

I shook my head. I didn't mind as long as she was quiet. I gave her one of my tickets.

Her stomach was huge. She had to lean back to balance. She waddled when she walked. The baby was pressing on her bladder and her lungs. It was hard for her to breathe, let alone talk. The air was sticky. She gasped like a fish, reached out and held on to my shoulder. 'Stop, Tom.'

We stopped by the gorillas. There was a large male – a silverback – who lay asleep in a corner. There were two young black-backs. There was an adult female. She was called Zanzi. She squatted with her nose against the bars, wiping the stinging barbs off a sprig of nettle with her leathery fingers.

She was watching my mother. My mother was too tired to notice, but I did. The gorilla was gazing at my mother's belly. It was a know-ing stare. It was as if she could see through the fabric of my mother's dress, through her stretched, blue-veined skin and her aching bands of muscle right into the soft, red lining of her womb.

My mother leaned on the rails. Her eyes were closed. I crouched down. My movement distracted the gorilla and her small amber eyes met mine. She cleared her throat to make sure she had my full attention, then she signed to me. I swear on my mother's life. She was using sign language. She cradled her own enormous belly in her hands and she signed, 'Gorilla Seed.' She drew her lips back into a shy smile and hooted softly. She signed again in case I hadn't quite got the message. This time, she used different signs: 'Baby here too.'

I didn't tell anyone Zanzi's secret. That was the way she wanted it. She didn't have much privacy either. I knew what that was like and it was the least I could do.

Even the zookeeper didn't know she was pregnant. It is hard to tell if a female gorilla is going to have a baby because they nearly always have pot bellies. People think they're fat because they're lazy and all they do is eat and sleep. That's not true. That's the shape they're meant to be. They eat leaves and roots and flowers. They're plant eaters. Plant food takes a long time to digest. It stays packed inside. That's why they have such big stomachs.

Inside Zanzi, the baby gorilla was growing. I wondered how big it was, compared to the one inside my mother. It takes nine months before a human baby is ready to be born. It's eight and a half months for a gorilla – almost the same. Our genes are almost identical. Almost. How much difference does 'almost' make?

My little sister was born a week later during a thunderstorm. That morning, my mother scrubbed the floor, tipped out drawers and ironed tiny clothes. She washed windows, vacuumed under beds and polished things that weren't dusty. She filled a bucket with hot water and started to wash down the walls in the kitchen. She was exhausted. My father took the bucket and told her to sit down.

'Leave me alone!' she said. 'I'm nesting.'

That same morning, Zanzi built a nest. I watched her through the bars. The only building material she had was straw. She didn't think that was good enough. She pushed her arm through the gaps in the bars and plucked at the sticky wild grasses that grew up through the low hedge. When no one was looking, I pulled up some tall bedding plants with broad leaves and pushed them into the enclosure.

She looked at me under her eyelashes and took them. She sniffed the sappy ends. She walked on two feet with the plants under her arm and grabbed a thick rope with her free hand. She swung up to a high wooden platform, gathered some straw around her and began to bend and weave the plants into a bowl shape.

The silverback, Congo, came to see what she was doing. He grabbed one of the bedding plants and sucked at a bright-red flower that burst from the end of a woody stem.

Zanzi screamed at him and slapped the wooden platform. Leave me alone! I'm nesting.

He grunted, rolled the flower in his lips and left.

I left too. It was a hot, breathless night. Hailstones rattled against my window. Thunder boomed. Lightning cracked. It was Night Music, composed for giving birth. My mother joined in with the chorus. I'd heard it before, way back before I was born. Vixen bark. Whale sob. Cow moo. I love that piece of music because it has no words.

My baby sister slid out of my mother before she could get to hospital. She was born on the hall floor. I came downstairs and saw her curled up like a bud on my mother's breast. She was still attached to the cord. She was covered in creamy wax and blood. She didn't cry. My father did. When he stopped, he couldn't speak. He was struck dumb.

They called her Daisy. It suited her. When

she was washed, she was so new and fresh she seemed more like a flower than a person. She had petals for fingers. There were no pores in her skin. When I stroked her cheek I couldn't be sure if I was touching her or not, she was so soft, so plumped.

She couldn't speak of course. Not yet. But she signed. No one else noticed. They were too busy, too tired. They didn't realize she was trying to tell them something. She was very patient with them. She would sign over and over again. Sucking her fists. Drawing up her knees. Squeezing her eyes shut. She became exhausted, trying to explain herself over and over again and then she would cry. It was a last desperate measure.

If she cried, someone would pick her up. They became irritable, trying to guess what was wrong. Was she wet? Was she hot? Was she hungry? She would cry louder. She was crying because she wanted to be held. That's what she'd asked for. Not to be fed. Not to be played with. Not to be undressed. No wonder babies cry so much.

Zanzi's baby didn't cry. She was born on the same night as Daisy, with the scent of hot rain in the trees and the leopard roar of thunder. A little patch of rainforest in the city zoo. Zanzi cleaned the baby and wore it on her chest like a brooch. She stroked it while it suckled. She mustn't sleep for fear of python. For fear of panther. They might take her baby. Congo would protect her when he woke. Congo was the father.

The young black-backs were not allowed to touch Zanzi. That was gorilla law. In the wild, they would have left and started their own families by now. It wasn't possible here. There was a housing crisis.

This was Zanzi's first baby. She would have to look after it alone, with no aunties or sisters to help. There had been another female gorilla called Kolo, but Kolo died last winter. She hadn't been replaced. She was only thirteen.

In the zoo, Kolo could have lived until she was fifty. In the wild, she'd have died young. Killed for bush-meat or caught in a poacher's snare. She might have had her head and hands cut off for trophies. Her forest might have been chopped into firewood by people who also had nowhere to call home. Now the gorillas were refugees, just like the humans. Our genes are almost identical. Almost.

If a wild gorilla was lucky, it died of old age. By its thirty-fifth birthday, it would have lost its teeth and slowly starved to death. Kolo was born in captivity. Her chances for a long life should have been good. She had the best medical and dental care in the world, but she had no immune system to fight off the disease she caught from a human. It soon killed her. Zoo gorillas are fragile. When they are sick, they give up. They lose the will to live. Ape suicide.

Zanzi was ten. She was happy and well. She had her back to the bars when I arrived.

I was early, the first through the gate. I

clicked my tongue softly and she turned around.

She was nursing a baby in her lap. It was much smaller than Daisy. Two kilograms at the most. Hair grew in fine tufts from its pinkish-grey skin. It had pink spots on the soles of its feet. It stopped suckling and gazed up at its mother with huge caramel eyes.

Zanzi chuckled. She took her hand away from underneath the infant and let it cling to her fur. She looked at me and signed, 'My baby.'

I signed back. 'She is beautiful.'

Even if she didn't understand the meaning of the words, she could read my feelings. She saw that the sight of her child had made my eyes sparkle and my mouth split into a smile so wide she could see my teeth. 'Beautiful,' she signed.

Eric the gorilla keeper came and stood next to me. Zanzi backed off. She swung on her rope, then climbed right up to her wooden platform with the baby under one arm.

'Hard to tell if they're pregnant,' he said, 'with their pot bellies. Fantastic news!'

The news spread fast. A sign went up outside the zoo: 'Come and see the baby gorilla!' Within minutes there was a crowd around the enclosure, pushing and shoving and climbing on to the low wall to try to see the baby.

Zanzi hunched herself up on the platform and threw straw over her shoulder. She was agitated. The crowd grew louder until there was a shrieking wall of flesh right around the enclosure. I willed them to shut up for her sake and for the baby's. But they wouldn't.

'Come down, Zanzi.'

'Here, Zanzi!'

'Show us your baby!'

Cameras flashed. People banged on the bars. Eric told them to stop, but no one heard him. He was powerless against the mass. Clang, clang, clang. They couldn't just be quiet and watch. They couldn't come in peace.

They came as a pack. Almost, but not quite human.

The press arrived. The television camera crews. Still Zanzi wouldn't come down from her platform. The Zoo Chief spoke to Eric. The camera crew had a crane. If the gorilla wouldn't come down, they would go up and get an aerial shot. The zoo needed the publicity – the money.

Eric was instructed to lock the door to the gorillas' inner enclosure. It could be locked automatically from the outside. It was their only bolt hole. The television crew would set up another camera there. One way or another, they would capture that baby.

I watched the crane rise. As soon as the camera was in position, Zanzi swung away on the rope. She raced for the bolt hole. It was locked. She thumped and thumped, calling out in dismay. She hurled herself at the closed shutters. Congo walked out from behind a grassy mound to see what was going on. He drew himself up on to his knuckles and stared at the camera crew. He shook his massive head from side to side, slapped the ground and threw sticks. The crowd laughed. They beat their own chests in mockery.

He stopped bluffing. He pulled back his lips and charged at the bars. The vibration of his roar shook the enclosure. The crowd screamed and surged back. A TV camera was smashed in the crush. The Zoo Chief panicked.

Eric was furious in his own quiet way. He asked the crane driver to leave. He cordoned off the gorilla enclosure with a barrier of plastic cones and red-and-white tape.

Deeply ashamed, he unlocked the bolt hole. Zanzi crawled inside.

I went home feeling angry and frustrated. I wanted to speak up for Zanzi but I couldn't. When I saw her trying to protect her baby from the mob, I didn't see a gorilla and its child; I saw Mum and Daisy. After Daisy was born, the phone kept ringing and ringing. People kept knocking on the door and coming in and out. In and out. Talking, talking, talking.

They all wanted to have a piece of Daisy.

They woke her up so they could hold her when she desperately needed to sleep. She was worn out already. She was still getting used to the feel of air in her lungs, the sharp stabs of sunlight in her eyes.

My mother let the visitors hold her, but she didn't want them to. Not yet. She couldn't bear to be apart from Daisy. She needed to hold her and smell her. Be skin to skin with her. Feel her soft weight against her body even though the cord had been cut.

Every time she had to hand Daisy over, her lips went into a thin, nervous smile. This was her baby – hers to touch alone – but there was no getting away from people. A new baby was public property. Mum would sit on the edge of the sofa, ready to spring, in case anyone dropped her.

I wanted to put up barriers, like Eric. I wanted to fetch plastic cones and run red-and-white tape all round our house and put up signs: Do Not Pass Barrier. Do Not Disturb.

The visitors talked about me in front of me.

'Does Tom like the baby?'

Normally that would make my mother angry. Normally she would say, 'Why don't you ask him? He's not deaf, you know.' She didn't do that now. She was too busy trying to defend Daisy. I was no longer seen as the help-less one.

'Yes. He's very good with her.'

All of them wanted to know if the baby would be able to talk, but they never quite fin-ished their sentences. They made my mother do it for them. Forced her into facing the fact that this baby might also be faulty in some way.

'Will she be able to . . . ?'

'It must be hard to tell yet, but . . . ?'

'Have they tested her for . . . ?'

My father was in the kitchen doing the washing-up. He pushed himself up on his knuckles on the edge of the sink, shook his head and stared at the visitors through the open door. He threw knives and forks around and slapped the table. He charged into the other room. 'It's too early to tell,' he barked.

The guests fell silent. They finished their tea and left. Dad put the answerphone on. Mum crawled upstairs to bed in tears and went to sleep with Daisy on her chest.

Things improved for both mothers after a while. The novelty of the new babies soon wore off. Neighbours who never usually spoke to us stopped turning up out of the blue when we were trying to eat a late lunch and the arrival of a litter of lion cubs took the attention away from the baby gorilla.

When Eric felt sure that Zanzi had relaxed into motherhood, a national newspaper was invited to send one photographer to the zoo to take a picture of the baby gorilla. The zoo had christened her Zoe, but Zanzi never called her that, she called her Beautiful. She had a name for me too. I told her I was Tom, but it meant nothing to her. 'You Sky Eyes,' she signed.

Beautiful grew twice as fast as Daisy. Her skin turned dusky, the pink spots disappeared and her skinny limbs grew strong. The little wisps of hair grew thick and fluffy right over her head and down to her knuckles. Her face, her palms and the soles of her feet stayed bare.

Zanzi rolled her baby round and round in her lap. It hiccuped and burped and sucked its toes. It sat up and explored its fur. Daisy couldn't sit up yet. I could thread her finger through the handle of a rattle, but she couldn't grip it. Not properly. There was nothing wrong with her – she just wasn't a gorilla. Not quite.

Eric often used to stand by me while I watched Zanzi. He loved the gorillas, I could see that. He was a quiet, thoughtful man. He would stand there in silence for ages, as if he were building up to something. Then he would talk in short bursts. I think he was mostly talking to himself. He never seemed to expect a reply. A nod or a smile was enough from me. In that way, we almost had a conversation. He wasn't even aware that I couldn't talk.

'They make over twenty-five different sounds, do gorillas,' he said, 'yet they can't reproduce human speech. They haven't got the hardware . . . pity, that.'

I nodded and smiled. He told me the vervet monkeys had the most advanced system of communication in the natural world. He seemed disappointed. It was a competition he wanted the great apes to win. They were his favourites: chimpanzees, orang-utans, gorillas.

'They do say they can learn sign language,' he said. 'There was one called Koko, who lived at the Gorilla Foundation in California. Learned over eight-hundred signs by all accounts.' He laughed softly to himself. 'They say she even told jokes.'

Zanzi dangled her baby in the air and swung it to and fro. It cooed and gurgled like a toddler having its first swing at the park.

'This fellow, Chomsky,' Eric mused, 'he studied the apes who used sign language and he reckoned they didn't know what they were talking about. Not really.'

He leaned sideways on the railings and sneezed, then he took his glasses off and polished them on his handkerchief. There was a purple dent on the bridge of his nose. Zanzi signed to me behind his back.

'Wet-elephant noise! Pebble-face.'

Eric turned back and she pretended to scratch her armpit. It was hard not to laugh out loud. She called him Pebble-face! The thick lenses in his glasses were pebbles. His sneeze reminded her of an elephant! She smacked her lips and grinned.

'Can gorillas talk?' Eric pondered. 'Humans can fly about ten metres. That's what they do in the Olympics. Is that flying? The question is meaningless. Anyway, that's what Chomsky said.'

I frowned and shook my head.

'He may be right, he may be wrong,' said Eric, 'but this I do know: gorillas are as sharp as razors . . . Be seeing you.'

Wet-elephant noise Pebble-face walked off. I nodded and waved goodbye.

I asked Ruth about Koko. She said she'd read about her. She'd heard of Chomsky, the linguist. I asked her what she thought. As a speech therapist, did she think apes could really understand sign language? Was it possible?

'Not sure,' she signed. 'They might just be copying to please their trainers or to get a reward. What do you think, Tom?'

'I think they understand more than we think.'

'Why?'

I told her about Zanzi. How she told me she was pregnant. How she called me Sky Eyes. 'Gorillas can see in colour, Ruth.'

Maybe Zanzi didn't know the sign for *blue* so she used *sky* to describe the colour of my eyes.

Ruth smiled. 'That's incredible.'

I wasn't sure if she thought it was unbelievable or amazing. She didn't dismiss it though.

The next time I went to see her, she told me she'd found something out for me.

'Read this, Tom.'

It was a paper from the Washington University of Chimpanzee and Human Communication. I began to read it silently to myself. The institute was home to a family of five chimps who, according to their trainers, had all mastered sign language.

'Try and read it out loud, Tom. What's this word? Ch . . . ch . . .'

One of the longest recorded sentences made by a chimp contained seven signs. Sometimes, the baby chimpanzees picked up sign language by watching their own mothers . . .

'Tom, say "chimp". Come on, Ch . . . ch . . .'

An important finding was that chimps could create new signs by combining others. One chimp described a watermelon as 'drink fruit'.

'Tom!'

I wouldn't say chimp. I wouldn't even try. Maybe this was what it was like for the apes at the University of Chimpanzee and Human Communication.

'Say "Human!", Koko.'

'Come on, Tom. You can do it.'

Ruth was really getting on my nerves. I lost my temper with her.

'Shut up, Pig-face! Stop treating me like a monkey.'

I walked out of the classroom.

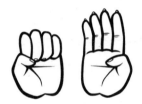

At three months old, Beautiful had her first teeth. Ruth came to the zoo with me. I was sorry I had called her Pig-face. I was just sick of being ordered to speak. I didn't have the hardware.

'You do,' she said. 'I believe you can talk. One day you will talk, Tom.'

I don't know why she believed in me like that, but she did. I can tell if people are lying.

It is so easy to tell. They sweat a little and talk too fast. They scratch their noses. Look at their feet. They fiddle. Sometimes they try and double bluff and look you straight in the eye, but they always hold the gaze too long, like bad actors.

Taking Ruth along meant I had to use up two of my tickets. I didn't have many left. She offered to pay, but I wanted to take her to show how sorry I was for being rude. She was only trying to help – it was just such a crass way of doing it. I felt tricked into trying to speak. She'd even highlighted the word 'chimp' in fluorescent yellow pen. Like I was blind as well as dumb. She might as well have gone the whole way and offered me a peanut as a reward.

'I'm sorry,' she said. 'I just thought if it was something you were interested in—'

'Ruth.'

'I know . . . patronizing.'

*

Zanzi was sitting on her wooden platform when we arrived. When she saw me, she picked her baby up and swung down on the rope to see me.

'This is my friend,' I signed.

Zanzi sat down and picked her nose. I tried again. I put my arm around Ruth to prove it.

'Friend of Sky Eyes . . . Say "Hello".'

She picked up a piece of straw and sucked it loudly. She wasn't going to talk to me.

'Say Pebble-face!'

She shook her head and chattered her teeth. I felt angry with her.

'Never mind,' Ruth said. 'Maybe she doesn't feel like talking. You understand that feeling, don't you?'

Ruth was only short. She had to kneel on the low wall to get a better look at the baby. It was trying to crawl. There was a white tuft on its backside. Eric said all baby gorillas had a white tuft. It was to warn the other gorillas to be gentle with them. Ruth's eyes filled up.

'Ah, she's gorgeous! What's her name?'

'Zoe.'

'Beautiful,' signed Zanzi.

I grabbed Ruth's arm and shook it.

'Did you see that? Did you see what Zanzi signed just then?'

She missed it. She was too busy cooing to the baby.

'Oh, *Ruth*!'

'What? Did she do it? What did she say?'

'It doesn't matter. Maybe I was imagining it.'

'Damn,' said Ruth.

We stayed and watched them for half an hour. Ruth tried to sign to Zanzi to see if she would say 'Beautiful' again, but she wouldn't. She wasn't in the mood. We went to see the other animals. Ruth wanted to see the tiger, but it was pacing up and down against the glass. Up and down. Up and down. She came away.

'It's going mad in there,' she said. 'You can

see it in its eyes.'

I checked. She was right. The flame had gone out. It made me want to cry. We went to the aviary. There was a small crowd gathered around one of the cages. An old man was having a conversation with a grey parrot.

'Hello, matey!'

'Hello, matey!'

The parrot gripped the bars with its claws and beak and whistled loudly.

'Cheeky!' said the old man.

'Cheeky, cheeky, cheeky!'

Ruth said it wasn't a real conversation.

'It's just mimicking,' she said.

Say 'chimp' Tom. Ch . . . ch . . . come on, you can do it.

'Parrots don't understand what they are saying, Tom.'

'Goodbye!' said the old man.

'Hello, matey!'

Compared to Zanzi's baby, Daisy was really

lagging behind. At six months, she was much smaller. She was still bald and pretty helpless. She was sitting up, but she still fell backwards if she was startled. She couldn't talk, of course. She was too young. She wouldn't be able to talk until she was over a year old. That's how it was with human babies.

Not in my case though. Daisy was already babbling. I loved to hear her doing that. I asked my mother if I babbled, once. She said yes, but I'm not sure she could remember.

'I'm sure you did,' she said. 'In fact, you even said "dada".'

'Not "mama"?' I signed.

'No, not that.'

She had never heard me say 'mama'. Daisy would be the first to say that. I pressed my lips together . . . Mmmmm . . . but it wouldn't come. It just wouldn't come.

I had only three tickets left. They were supposed to last me a whole year. Even so, I couldn't keep away. I'd have to ask for some more for my birthday.

'Just going out, Mum.'

'To the zoo again?'

'To see the gorillas.'

I'd told her all about Beautiful. Every time Daisy learned something new, I would tell her, 'Zanzi's baby can already do that.'

She would laugh and say that Zanzi's baby sounded very advanced. She could walk now. She couldn't do it straight away. First, she learned to crawl. Then, when she could do that, she started pulling herself up on the rubber tyre or she'd hold on to the bars and totter along. When she let go, her legs used to buckle and she would fall down hard on her white tuft. Not any more.

'Just like when you learned to walk,' my mother said.

Daisy wasn't very playful yet, but Beautiful was. She would climb all over Congo, biting him and jumping on him. She would pull his hair when he was sleeping and poke twigs up his nose. He was endlessly patient. He grumbled a bit, but he never smacked her. He just rolled his eyes.

Zanzi still gave her milk, but now she was starting to chew leaves. She was going on to solids. My mother mashed up bananas for Daisy. Daisy was suspicious at first. She pushed the banana back out with her tongue. I saw Beautiful do the same thing with a grape. She found it in the grass. She kept putting it in her mouth, spitting it out, sniffing it then putting it back in. When she finally bit through the skin, the sudden sensation of juice squirting into the back of her throat made her leap into the air.

'Has she got any brothers or sisters?' my mother asked.

'Not yet. She's Zanzi's first baby.'

Gorillas usually have their first baby between the ages of eight and ten. Eric told me that. The second baby might not come along for another three years and twins were very rare. The mother gorilla might have several babies in her lifetime, but half of them died. Mum said it used to be like that for human babies. Her great-grandmother had thirteen children, but only seven survived.

I went to the zoo early. The whole house wakes when Daisy wakes. I had my breakfast and left. Mum gave me some money to buy something to eat. I thought I'd save it and put it towards another ticket just in case no one bought me any.

I went to see Zanzi. I couldn't spot her at first. Congo was there. The black-backs were sunbathing behind a crate, but I couldn't see her. Maybe she was asleep in the inner enclosure. It wasn't like her though. She liked to sleep outside. I wished I could call out her name. 'Z . . . z . . .' But it wouldn't come. Just a low hiss. I saw Eric.

'Looking for Zanzi? She's hiding. Not very happy, I'm afraid.'

Eric didn't look very happy either. He

sucked his cheeks in and shrugged. He wouldn't look at me. I opened my mouth, as if I was going to ask him a question. He shook his head, unwilling to speak. I signed to him.

'What's wrong?'

He looked at me, surprised.

'Sorry, I didn't know you were deaf.'

I signed again, hoping he could work out what I was trying to say. It wasn't that difficult. A gorilla could do it.

'I'm not deaf. I just can't speak. Why is Zanzi sad?'

He held his hands up. 'Sorry. I don't understand.'

I walked round the enclosure. I still couldn't see her. I stood by the bars and waited. After ten minutes, I saw the straw moving. Zanzi lay on her belly under the straw with her arms and legs tucked under her. She lifted her head up for a few seconds. Her eyes were empty and dull. She looked like she'd been drugged.

Beautiful had gone.

I double-checked. I stood on the wall and edged all the way round. What could have happened to Beautiful? Maybe she'd had an accident. Maybe she'd tried to swing on a rope and lost her grip. Maybe she'd fallen and broken her neck. But baby gorillas are strong! Shortly after they are born they can support their own weight hanging from one hand for up to three minutes.

Congo sat with his back to the bars. If he was upset, he didn't show it. In the wild, an outsider silverback sometimes came and killed a baby gorilla in an attempt to mate with its mother – but there was no threat of that here. Not in the city zoo.

Would the young black-backs have harmed Zanzi's child? It seemed unlikely. They were too afraid of Congo. He was in charge. Anyway, Zanzi let the juvenile gorillas touch the baby now. They were gentle with her. In a few months, she would be off playing with them. Wrestling and climbing. Joining in with their rowdy games.

I came back to the place where Zanzi was crouched under the straw. She hadn't moved. I signed to her: 'Talk to me, Zanzi. Where is Beautiful? Where is she?'

Zanzi let out a deep, human-like sigh and closed her eyes. I waited silently for half an hour. She opened her eyes again and sat up. Suddenly alert, she looked around desperately for her baby, then remembered it had gone. Very slowly, she held up her fingers and thumbs and tried to tell me what had happened.

'Baby gone.'

I asked her where? 'Baby gone where? Tell Sky Eyes!'

'Sting-sleep.'

Sting-sleep? What did she mean, sting-sleep? Sting . . . sting like an insect? Beautiful had been stung? What, by a bee or a wasp? A hornet? Maybe she'd had an allergic reaction. Maybe she'd picked up a piece of peach with a drowsy wasp on it and the wasp had stung her. Her throat had swollen up so badly, she'd choked and died. But if that had happened, then why hadn't Eric told me? I'd read his face. It said guilt, not sorrow. No, the sting-sleep hadn't happened to the baby, it had happened to Zanzi. She told me so.

'Pebble-face. Sting-sleep.'

Pebble-face! I was right! Eric had something

to do with the disappearance of Beautiful.
Sting-sleep . . . what would sting apart from an
insect? An injection! Zanzi had been given an
injection. Hit with a tranquillizer dart. That
was it! She'd been put to sleep and when she
woke up . . .

'Baby gone.'

She slumped back down in the straw and
hid her face. She went back to sleep. I stayed
with her. While she slept, her face contorted in
dreams. She whimpered and barked. Python
nightmares. Leopard terrors. She would wake
herself up and look around for Beautiful all
over again, searching the straw, tossing it in the
air. Then she would remember – baby gone.
Milk ran down her fur like a broken string of
pearls. Her whole body was weeping. I cried
with her. It upset her more. She called me
Rain-face.

'She'll be all right in a bit,' Eric said. 'The
milk will dry up. She'll get over it.'

I don't think he believed it any more than I

did. He removed the baby's photograph. He slid it out of the metal and plastic panel which was attached to the rail. I'd read it a hundred times.

Welcome, Zoe, the new zoo baby!

Birth date: 6.6.04
Weight: 1.8 kg
Mother's name: Zanzi
Father's name: Congo
Species: Western Lowland Gorilla
Subspecies: Gorilla gorilla gorilla

'All part of the breeding programme,' Eric said. 'Can you hear me by the way?'

I nodded and dried my eyes on my sleeve.

'I don't like this any more than you do,' he said. 'Other zoos need gorillas. I just do what I'm told.'

So Beautiful wasn't dead. She had been taken away from Zanzi to be sent to another zoo. It was too cruel. She was far too young. It didn't make sense.

'We can't take any more out of the wild,' Eric said. 'They'll be extinct in twenty years if we do – maybe sooner.'

He gave me the photograph. 'Want to keep it? To remember Zoe by?'

My eyes welled up again. He brushed an invisible speck off his jacket and pretended he hadn't noticed.

'Zoe will be fine. She'll be adopted by another female in America.'

Where was she now? Surely she wasn't in America already?

I signed to Eric as simply as I could. I had to know. 'Where baby?'

He looked away.

I squeaked and grunted, trying to squeeze it out in proper speech. 'Whuh . . . buh . . . buh?'

He shook his head. I was embarrassing him. 'Sorry, son.'

I followed him secretly back to the Keepers'

Lodge. I wondered if he'd taken Beautiful there. Maybe he'd drawn off some of Zanzi's milk while she was tranquillized and put it in a bottle for the baby. My mother had an electric pump that she used to collect milk for Daisy so my father could feed her if she had to go out. Daisy was almost weaned now, but Beautiful wasn't. Gorillas aren't weaned until they're at least two years old. She wouldn't last all the way to America without any milk.

Eric turned round and saw me. 'What now? I've given you the picture.'

I looked through the open door into his lodge.

'Oh, I get you,' he said. 'No, she's not in here . . . go on.' He took his keys out of his pocket, hung them on a rack and closed the door.

It started to rain. I went back to see Zanzi. She sat there miserably, sucking rain water off her fur.

'Baby not dead,' I signed. Her expression

didn't change. She didn't understand. She worked her fingers together. I thought she was just wriggling them at first, but she kept repeating the action. Trying to tell me something.

'Worm food. Baby gone.'

Worm food. Her sign for death. She thought Beautiful was dead. She couldn't have wandered off, Zanzi knew that. She knew every inch of the enclosure. There was no escape. But a snake could have come. A snake could squeeze through the bars. A leopard could have come while she slept. She heard the leopard roaring every day. Every night. She couldn't see it, but then you never saw the leopard. Not until he pounced. She always knew it might come. Leopards must creep through gorillas' dreams like monsters crawl through mine. But Beautiful wasn't dead.

'Not worm food,' I signed.

She slapped the muddy grass with her palm.

I told her again. 'Not worm food. Pebble-face take baby.'

She looked at me curiously. She made the sign for Pebble-face and showed her canines. They were huge. Bone yellow. She looked nothing like Zanzi when she pulled that face. She looked like a demon. Loathsome. Malevolent. She grabbed a handful of dung and hurled it at the bars. It shattered. She signed with smeared hands.

'Pebble-face dung ball.'

She was swearing at him. She shook her head from side to side then wiped her palms carefully on the grass. She hung her head and picked at her nails. She hugged herself and rocked. She was Zanzi again. Gentle, heartbroken Zanzi. She plucked at the fur on her arm. She plucked until there was a bald patch. She scratched it obsessively until it bled.

'Don't, Zanzi.'

She wouldn't stop. I was sure Beautiful must still be in the zoo. She had to be. Sometimes they blacked out the glass in the cages. Perhaps she was in one of those. Or in an isolation cage in the zoo hospital. Wherever she was, I would find her. Zanzi tasted the blood on her arm with her tongue and sighed. She whimpered and slapped her forehead.

'Where baby, Sky Eyes?'

'I don't know. I will look for her. I will find her.'

I backed away from her cage. She was signing in the rain, over and over. Where baby? Where baby? Where baby? As soon as I was out of sight, she started to wail. The sound echoed all around the zoo. The chimpanzees heard it and began to shriek in sympathy. The lar gibbons sang a haunting dirge and flew through the dripping trees like fuzzy ghosts. Baboons barked and the mandrill boomed.

The message crossed over the species. The cow elephants heard it and went down on their knees. The giraffes swivelled their ears and lowered their delicate heads. Even the turtle – the silent turtle – felt the vibrations in the thick, salt water of her tank and searched in vain for somewhere to lay her eggs. Over and over and over again.

Above all this, I heard the constant, dreadful wailing of Zanzi. The last time I heard it was at my grandmother's funeral. It was the sound of my own mother grieving. It wasn't a human sound. Not quite. It was older than that. As old as death itself. If you listened hard enough above the noise of life, you could hear it. Sense it. It was always there.

Beautiful heard it. She called out. That's how I found her.

I heard her call, but I couldn't get to her. The baby gorilla was in a small, portable cage in the back room of the old insect house. It was the room where they used to hatch out the insect larvae. There used to be shelves full of clear plastic boxes filled with eggs the size of pinheads arranged on pads of white kitchen paper. There were jars filled with caterpillars no thicker than threads of cotton. Jars which held chrysalises woven on to twigs All these things had gone.

The building had been emptied of beetles, spiders and butterflies. There was nothing left to see. The doors were closed to the public. I squeezed round the side of it, stood on a bucket and looked through the small, dirty window. I saw Beautiful through a gap in the blinds. She was quiet now. Someone was in the room with her – a man in green overalls. He took a bottle out of a microwave and tipped a few drops of milk on to his wrist. He poked the teat through the wire on the front of the cage. Beautiful wouldn't take it. She shuffled into a corner and sucked her fingers.

The man sat down and talked to someone on the telephone. I lost my footing on the bucket and he saw me. He rapped on the window.

'Private property!' he shouted.

I ran off. Zanzi was still wailing in the rain. I avoided her. I left the zoo by another route.

I'd said I would find her baby. I couldn't face seeing her without it. She wouldn't understand, she would feel betrayed. I would be a dung ball like Pebble-face.

I walked home. On the way, I wondered what I could do to help Zanzi. Eric said there was nothing he could do. He just did as he was told. It was all part of the breeding programme.

Aren't we all, though? When human tribes are threatened with extinction, do we snatch their babies and send them to America? Maybe that's exactly what happens. Who knows?

What I knew for certain was this: Zanzi loved her baby every bit as much as my mother loved Daisy. My mother was lucky. She had two children to love and hold. She had her arms full. Zanzi's were empty. I had two tickets left.

I was soaked through by the time I got in. I went straight to my room and changed into dry clothes. I knew I didn't have much time. I prayed the sun would come out. For a while, it did. I offered to take my sister out in her pram. Mum was grateful. She needed a rest. Daisy could do with some fresh air. 'Just take her round the block,' she said.

I pushed the pram round the block. Down the high street. Up the hill to the zoo. There was no queue. It was late afternoon. I pushed Daisy through the members' gate and handed over my two tickets. The woman in the kiosk gave me one back.

'Babies are free,' she said.

Beautiful wasn't free. She was trapped in a cage. She was being guarded. There was no way I could get her out. I hoped she was still there. I hoped the van hadn't already come to take her to the airport. They would do that after the zoo closed, so no one knew. People would protest if they knew a baby had been taken from its mother. People who had voices would protest. That's what I would do if I had a voice.

I parked Daisy in front of the pigs. A great swollen sow was lying on her side with twelve suckling piglets clamped on to her. There was no room for the thirteenth piglet. None of the others would move over. It squealed and squealed but no one took any notice. It gave up after a while and lay down by itself. Sometimes it doesn't matter how much you squeal, you don't always get your way. Noise is no good without cunning.

The pigpen was near the Keepers' Lodge. I wasn't really watching the pigs, I was watching the lodge. I saw Eric come out. He closed the door, but he didn't lock it. I turned and faced the pigs. He walked straight past me. He didn't even see me. I pushed the pram nearer to the lodge. Using it to shield me, I pushed the door open and grabbed the keys. I put them in my jacket. I knew which ones to grab. They were all marked.

I left the pram outside the aquarium along with several other pushchairs. Pushchairs weren't allowed inside. I took Daisy out of her pram and carried her to the gorilla enclosure. Congo was asleep. The black-backs were inside.

Zanzi was sitting in a corner by herself. I showed her Daisy. She turned her head away at first, but I knew she wouldn't be able to resist. After a few moments, she turned back to look at my sister and I asked her to do something for me. 'You hold baby.'

Slowly she came over. She stared at Daisy and sniffed. She seemed disappointed. She threw her hands up. 'Where baby?'

She wanted Beautiful. I didn't have her. Her arms ached with emptiness. I tried to persuade her again. 'You hold baby.'

She wasn't sure what to do. She understood what I wanted her to do, but she hesitated. She peered at me shyly through her long brown fingers. I held Daisy nearer to the bars. She gurgled and spread out her small, creamy hands – hands with dimples where the knuckles should be. It started to rain again.

'Good girl. Hold baby,' I insisted.

Zanzi reached out cautiously. She pushed both hands through the bars in readiness.

'Yes . . . hold.'

There was a woman with a child near by. They hurried off to escape from the drizzle. No one saw me unlock the cage door. I went inside the enclosure and sat Daisy down by my feet with my back to the door. She wobbled and grasped at a straw.

Zanzi sidled over. For a moment her brow wrinkled and her eyes glittered strangely. I thought, Oh God, she is going to make her demon face. She will kill my sister for not being Beautiful. She will call Congo. Congo will kill my sister for not being his child!

Zanzi scooped Daisy up and cradled her in the crook of one arm. She touched her fat cheek with her almost-human fingers, brushed her small, fuzzy head with her lips.

'Peach,' she signed.

My face coloured with shame. I was

ashamed that I hadn't trusted her with my peachy little sister. I locked myself inside the enclosure. People were coming. Zanzi heard them too. She held Daisy in one arm and swung on the rope to her day nest, seven metres up on the wooden platform. I hid inside a cube of straw bales. I watched through the gold slits in the straw.

A family arrived to look at the gorillas. A woman with a baby in a sling. A man with a toddler on his shoulders. The toddler pointed up at the platform.

'See baby!' she said.

The father looked up. 'Where's the baby?'

'Up dere!'

The mother looked up. 'Where?'

The father shook his head. 'I can't see one.'

The toddler became angry, but she didn't know enough words to explain why. She could see Zanzi rolling Daisy around in her lap. Her father couldn't. He'd been looking for the wrong kind of baby and even then he didn't really look. He didn't really want to be there.

The toddler swung her feet in frustration and pulled his hair. 'Is baby! Is baby!'

'Don't kick. Stop it! Do you want me to put you down?'

The mother saw Daisy first. She gasped. 'There is a baby!'

'Is baby,' said the toddler. She turned her father's head by his ears. 'Is baby, look!'

The parents screwed up their faces in disbelief.

'It's a doll,' they told their angry child. 'It's just a doll.'

'No dolly!' cried the child.

Some tourists came with cameras and maps and rucksacks. They read all the information about the gorillas in the plastic panels and discussed them. They looked at Congo, asleep on his back. They tried to find the black-backs and the baby and seemed annoyed that they weren't on display. One of the party pointed up excitedly.

'Baby!' he said.

'A baby gorilla? Where?'

'No, no – a human baby. I saw it move.'

His friends laughed. It's just a doll! Even the British wouldn't put a human baby in with a gorilla. Don't make us laugh!

High up on the platform, Daisy yawned and began to cry. She wasn't frightened or in pain. She wasn't hungry. That was her tired cry. I knew that. Zanzi knew that – so she rocked her, but people didn't understand. Visitors who were making their way to see the lions or the bears came over to see what all the shouting was about.

'The gorilla has stolen a baby! It's shaking it to death!'

Eric would hear them. He would be here soon. He would bring a dart-gun and take Daisy while Zanzi slept. Or would he? No, he couldn't risk it. He would be afraid she'd hurt the baby before the tranquillizer had time to work. It would be all his fault for leaving the lodge unlocked and letting a boy take the keys. They would bring in a marksman with a real gun. He would shoot Zanzi dead. A bullet through the brain.

I was trembling all over. I could hear the thumping of my own heart. It was shaking the straw. I pushed back the bales and stood up. People cried out, 'There's a boy!'

The others hadn't seen me yet. I grabbed hold of a rope.

'What boy? Where?'

'A boy on the rope!'

I ran as hard as I could and swung. I hit my back on the platform leg and nearly fell. I ran and swung again. This time, I caught my foot on one of the rungs. I climbed up and up.

'There's a boy climbing the platform!'

They had all seen me now. They were pointing. Pushing each other out of the way to get a better look.

'What's he doing?'

'Is he going to rescue the baby?'

'How did he get in there?'

Daisy had stopped crying. Zanzi held her to her chest and peered over the edge of the platform. I thought she might have helped me, but she didn't. She was wrapped up in Daisy.

I hauled myself up and sat near her. She ignored me. Maybe she thought I'd come to take Daisy back and she wasn't ready to part with her. Daisy wasn't her baby but maybe holding her made the emptiness less hollow. The ache less dull.

Congo twitched himself awake. He stretched slowly and sat up. He stared at the crowd. They went quiet. He sensed something was very wrong. He stood on his back legs and thumped his chest. Pok-pok-pok. He looked up and saw me. My stomach lurched. He started grunting. Giant, pig-like grunts. The crowd held its breath. With an ear-splitting bark, he went down on his knuckles and galloped sideways towards the base of the platform. He slapped the ground and began to climb up. Someone called my name. A woman screamed. It was my mother.

She'd found the pram by the aquarium. It was empty. She'd been looking for me everywhere. She guessed if I were anywhere, I'd be by the gorillas. She never guessed I'd be in with them. She'd heard the rumour as she ran from the aquarium.

'There's a boy inside the enclosure!'

She pushed her way to the front of the crowd and screamed. 'Tom . . . Tom!'

She didn't know Daisy was in there too. She had no idea where Daisy was. All she could see was Congo climbing up the platform towards her son and she screamed again, 'That's my son . . . my son!'

The crowd lowered their voices. They whispered low whispers. They lowered their voices to see if they could hear the old, old song of death. 'That's her son . . . her son!'

Congo kept climbing. Pebble-face came. I saw him out of the corner of my eye. I lay on my belly on the platform and made myself as small as I could. I folded my arms and legs under me, submitting to Congo. Showing him I was no threat. He sniffed my head. I could smell him.

I heard a fire engine. A police siren. My mother wailing, 'Tom!'

I could feel Congo's hot breath on the back of my exposed neck. Zanzi leaned forward. She thumped the platform and screamed in Congo's face. Back off! He was too close to her two new children – Sky Eyes and Peach. Back off!

I felt her fingers close round my waist. I felt myself move sideways, scraping the skin on my ankles on the rough, wet wood. She was pulling me close to her body. Protecting me.

She leaned forward and screeched louder. Congo snapped his head away as if he had been slapped round the face. He hung off the platform by his huge hand. She shouted again and he raced back down, humiliated. The shouting woke Daisy and she began to cry. My mother heard her. She looked around anxiously.

'Daisy?'

She pressed her face to the bars and looked up. For a moment she didn't say a word, then she became hysterical. She clambered on to the low wall and tried to climb the slippery bars. She kept sliding back down.

'Daisy!'

She couldn't begin to understand how Daisy

came to be there. I could see her trying to work it out. Perhaps she thought it was some kind of freak accident. It would never have crossed her mind that it was a deliberate act of mine. She was talking in gibberish.

'Tom Help God Daisy How?'

I was right. There would be no tranquillizing dart. Eight marksmen arrived. Four to target Zanzi. Four to target Congo. Gun barrels pushed through the bars. Eric had locked the black-backs inside the inner enclosure. I was glad about that. I was sorry I had put any of the gorillas at risk. Really sorry. I just couldn't see any other way.

The police moved the crowd behind a barrier. The crowd didn't want to move. They were annoyed that they no longer had such a good view. The marksmen continued to get into position. The press arrived. The television crews. They stood at the front, behind the barrier. The crowd complained bitterly. Now they couldn't see at all.

When everyone was assembled, I stood up. I stood up in front of Zanzi and spread my arms to protect her from the bullets. Nobody understood what I was doing. A policeman spoke through his loudhailer

'Tom. Do exactly as I say. Walk away slowly.'

I stayed where I was. They thought it was because I was scared, but I wasn't. I was being disobedient. Couldn't they see that? Were they really that stupid? I folded my arms.

'Tom. Walk away slowly. Move away from the gorilla.'

I shook my head. My mother pleaded with them to give her the megaphone.

'Tom. It's Mum. Do as they say!'

I shook my head. I held the keys up and rattled them. I could hear people mumbling.

'He stole the keys. He let himself into the cage!'

They started shouting up at me.

'What do you think you're doing?'

I wouldn't answer them and they didn't like that. They were angry with this reckless boy. They turned on my mother, as if she were to blame.

'What's the matter with him? Why won't he speak?'

My mother glared at them. She thumped the bars and screwed up her face.

'He can't!'

She went down on her knees on the low wall. I was sorry she had to suffer like that.

'Tom, I want Daisy back. I want my baby.'

'So does Zanzi!' I signed.

'What are you *saying*?' she wailed.

I held my hands above my head so everybody could see and I signed. Big, big gestures. 'They took Zanzi's baby away.'

A reporter climbed over the barrier. He pushed a microphone into my mother's face. 'What's he saying?' he asked. 'Tell us what he said!'

My mother breathed into the microphone.

The words were very faint. 'He said they took her baby away.'

I could hardly hear her, but a little girl at the front did. She whispered to her mother, 'They took the gorilla's baby away.'

The mother told the woman next to her, who turned and told the woman behind.

'They took the gorilla's baby away!'

Within seconds, the whisper grew louder and louder.

'They took the gorilla's baby away! They took the gorilla's baby away!'

They were protesting! Shouting the words for me! They jostled forward, jabbing their umbrellas in the air, disgusted that such a thing should be allowed to happen – that a baby had been taken away from its mother. The women became a dangerous force.

Even my mother got swept up in the tide. Desperate as she was, she realized what I was trying to do. She grabbed hold of Eric and shook him by the shoulders. 'What have you done with Zanzi's baby?'

Now it was personal. The gorilla had a name. Just like a person.

The crowd turned on Pebble-face and jeered, high-pitched, wild-faced, 'I bet it's wired up in a lab! They test things on gorillas because they're so like us!'

A woman crossed the barrier. She wanted to kill him. One of the marksmen swivelled his gun towards the crowd. I was afraid there would be a bloodbath. Things were falling apart. I tried to sign but no one was looking. I tried to sign, 'It's not Eric's fault! Not Eric!'

No one saw. They would rip Eric apart. I pressed my lips together.

'B . . . b . . .'

I closed my teeth and blew through them. Air puffed pathetically out of my mouth. I thought of Ruth.

'One day, you will talk, Tom.'

'B . . . beeee . . .'

She believed I could talk. If I was ever going

to, let it be now.

'Let it b . . . Let it bbbbb . . . Be quiiiiiiiii-iiiiet!'

Silence. Everyone was watching me . . . waiting. Beautiful was waiting. I heard my mother's voice. The words cracked when she said them, but she was insistent. 'Let him speak. Please . . . listen to Tom.'

Now for my master stroke. I took a deep breath. 'Don't . . . listen to m . . . me! Listen to h . . . listen to Zanzi!'

I stood aside. I was willing Zanzi to sign. I didn't know if she would. She was shy. She was upset. I pointed to my sister and signed. 'Is this your baby?'

Daisy lay in her arms. Zanzi blew softly on the thin covering of her blonde hair and ignored me. I tried again.

'This baby is not Beautiful! Where is Beautiful? Where is baby?'

Zanzi frowned. The crowd were stirring. The murmur went round.

'Shh . . . watch! He's talking to the gorilla in sign language.'

'What's he saying? What's *she* saying.'

Of course Zanzi wouldn't sign! She could sign with her own baby in her lap because it could cling to her fur. Daisy couldn't cling – if Zanzi let go, she would fall. She knew that.

'Give baby to Sky Eyes.'

'What's he saying?' asked the reporter.

My mother translated over the microphone. 'Give baby . . .'

I held out my hands to Zanzi. She didn't give Daisy back, she just let me take her from her arms without a struggle. She lowered her head.

'She gave him the baby!' muttered the crowd. 'He asked and she gave him the baby!'

I squatted down on the platform, propped Daisy between my knees and squeezed them together. It was a long, long way down. For a moment, I felt dizzy. My head swam.

'Is he OK? What's he doing? Why doesn't

he come down?'

I wasn't ready to come down. Seeing is believing. I wanted everyone to hear it from Zanzi.

I wanted them to see her in the paper. On the TV. I had to prove to them that it was wrong to take a gorilla's baby. Not because I said so, but because a gorilla did. I tried one last time. I turned to Zanzi. I put the signs together. I could hear the whirr of the cameras.

'Do you want your baby?'

I heard the hum of zoom lenses closing in on Zanzi's hands. She started to roll her fingers. A cameraman gave a thumbs-up. 'She's doing it. Go in closer . . .'

Go on, Zanzi. Go on. She stood up. She hooted softly and she put the three signs together. 'I want my baby.'

The crowd craned forward. 'What did she say?'

My mother spoke into the microphone. 'I want my baby.'

Now Zanzi couldn't stop. She thumped the platform. She held her head in her hands. She signed again and again. 'I want my baby! I want my baby! I want my baby.'

Now everybody knew. The gorilla had spoken. The crowd refused to leave until they gave her back her baby. The Zoo Chief tried to explain. 'It's part of the breeding programme. Our sister zoo in America needs a baby female gorilla. The mother gorilla is merely copying the boy. She doesn't know what she is saying.'

'Dung ball!' translated my mother.

The spokesman whipped round. Zanzi was signing at him furiously.

'Dung ball!' hissed the crowd. 'You're a dung ball! Give the gorilla her baby back!'

I was enjoying this. I held Daisy up and I shouted, 'S . . . swap you, Eric! Swap you!'

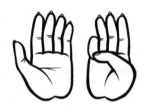

I refused to get down off the platform. I refused to give my mother's her baby back until Eric gave Zanzi hers. The Zoo Chief had no choice but to give in. It wasn't because he was moved by Zanzi's plight. Not really. I think he agreed because the zoo couldn't afford the bad publicity. Whatever the reason, we won.

By now, Zanzi had stopped signing. She

started her eerie wail again. She was losing patience. I was right next to her on the platform and the sound was deafening. I thought it would shake the nails out of the wood and the platform would collapse. Three of us dead. Beautiful orphaned. Imagine the ripples. They could bury us all together.

Women were crying. I could hear the sobs and the sound of the black-backs beating on the shutters of the inner enclosure. I could hear the elephant roar. The old, old song was starting up again. I moved my hand to the rhythm. I was the conductor, bringing in the orchestra – now the gibbons; now the giraffes.

Eric returned from the old insect house with the portable cage strapped to an electric trolley. The crowd hushed. They parted like the sea and he drove the trolley through the middle. He called up to me.

'Zoe's here, son. Stay where you are.'

I couldn't climb down with Daisy in my

arms anyway. The marksmen were still in position. Eric jumped off the trolley and unlocked
the little cage. He reached in and lifted
Beautiful out.

A grateful sigh went up. The wailing
stopped. The water in the turtle-tank stood
still.

The Zoo Chief unlocked the door to the
gorilla enclosure with a duplicate key. Eric
walked in with the baby gorilla on his hip. She
started squeaking and calling. Congo looked
up. I heard a trigger click. Eric kept walking.

I thought he was so brave. Not because
Congo or Zanzi might attack him, but because
if they put a foot wrong, they would be shot
dead. That would kill Eric. He loved his gorillas. It would be my fault if they were shot, but
he would blame himself. I was just a dumb boy.
He was the man in charge. Eric kept walking.
I could hear him talking softly.

'Good lad, Congo. Easy boy.'

Zanzi watched in disbelief as Pebble-face

started to climb the platform. I was afraid she would bite his face off. Snap his neck. I signed to her, 'Nice Pebble-face . . . baby coming!'

Eric climbed up slowly. He was an old guy. Beautiful was heavy. I reached out to try to help him up. 'I can manage,' he said. 'You little nutter.'

He was smiling though. He unwrapped the baby gorilla's arms from around his neck and pushed her up on to the platform. In a split second, Zanzi snatched the baby and slapped Eric's head. The slap must have hurt like mad, but he never shouted out. He just closed his eyes and winced until the pain passed. I think he thought he deserved it. Zanzi barked at us to leave her alone. She wanted to be alone with her child. I'd out-stayed my welcome.

'Coming down then?' Eric panted. 'Pass the baby. More trouble than they're worth.'

I hoped he was stronger than he looked.

'I won't drop her,' he said. 'I've got arms like

a gorilla. Come on.'

I gave him Daisy. She started crying. It was only her hungry cry. Eric sussed it straight away. 'What is it, feeding time?' he said.

He began to climb back down. I swung away on the rope. The crowd cheered. I'm not sure they were cheering for me. Not surprisingly, my mother didn't join in. Once she'd got over the bliss of having Daisy back in her arms, she went wild.

'What the hell have you got to say for yourself, Tom?'

'E . . . e . . . everything!' I shouted. I was totally unrepentant.

'What you did was unforgivable!' she yelled. And forgave me instantly.

Zanzi was in all the papers the next day. On the news programme on TV. So was I, of course. My father kept saying he couldn't believe it.

'Believe it!' I said.

The children in my class couldn't believe I could talk, but Ruth did. She'd always believed.

'All d . . . down to you,' I said.

She shook her head. 'No way. It was all down to you.'

It wasn't though. It was all down to Zanzi. There I was, trying to show her how to talk and she ended up teaching me.

I went back to see her shortly after that, on my very last ticket. I didn't have to ask if she was happy. It was obvious.

Pebble-face came and stood next to me. 'You've got a cheek,' he said, 'coming here.' But he wasn't cross.

I was worried he might have got the sack. He was too good a keeper to lose though. I liked Eric a lot. He wasn't really a dung ball.

'You do know Zoe will have to leave Zanzi one day?' he said.

I knew that. I asked him if she would be sent to the zoo in America. He nodded.

'When?'

'When she's six . . . don't have a go at me!'

I wasn't going to. Gorillas usually leave their mothers when they're about eight, but I reckon Eric did his best persuading America to wait that long.

By the time she was six, Beautiful would have lost her white tuft. She would be sleeping in her own nest. A couple of years after that she would be moving on anyway. Starting her own family. I could live with that and I reckoned Zanzi could too. She'd probably have another baby by then.

In six years' time, I would be seventeen.

I could go to America by myself and visit Beautiful. I would see how she was doing and come and report back to Zanzi.

I didn't know if Zanzi would ever forget Beautiful after she was gone. She seemed to have a pretty good memory. She knew a lot of signs that I never taught her. Maybe she learned them from her mother, whoever she was. I asked Eric.

'She was called Bulu,' he said. 'Zanzi was born in California.'

California? That's where the Gorilla Foundation is. The place where Koko came from – Koko who learned over 800 signs and told jokes! Maybe Koko knew Bulu. Maybe she showed Bulu how to sign and Bulu showed Zanzi.

Did Eric believe that mother gorillas could teach their babies how to communicate with humans?

'What you asking me for?' he said. 'If that's what you believe, ask Zanzi.'

I didn't need to. Just before closing time, when the zoo was almost empty and Eric had gone, I said my usual goodbyes to Zanzi. I was just walking away when I heard a soft hooting sound coming from the gorilla enclosure. I stopped and turned round.

It was Beautiful. She was working her fingers and thumbs. Her little brown hands were moving just like a human's. Almost like a gorilla's. She had something to say to me. 'Goodbye, Eye Sky.'

Well, we all have to learn.

RAT HEAVEN

A twisted rat's tale from Jeanne Willis, the author of *DUMB CREATURES*.

You wanted a pet you could talk to. One that came when you called its name. One that did tricks. You didn't want a rat, you wanted a dog! But you got me instead, and from the very first day we had a friendship made in heaven. Until Chelsea Brown came along – your new best friend. Now your life is full of sleepovers, lip-gloss and shopping. But is all that to die for?

What would I know anyway? I'm just a dirty rat . . .

A selected list of titles
available from Macmillan Children's Books

The prices shown below are correct at the time of going to press. However, Macmillan Publishers reserves the right to show new retail prices on covers which may differ from those previously advertised.

Rat Heaven	Jeanne Willis	1 405 02068 7	£7.99

Shock Shop

The Beast of Crowsfoot Cottage	Jeanne Willis	0 330 41569 7	£3.99
Stealaway	K. M. Peyton	0 330 39739 7	£3.99
The Bodigulpa	Jenny Nimmo	0 330 39750 8	£3.99
Wicked Chickens	Vivian French	0 330 41575 1	£3.99
Long Lost	Jan Mark	0 330 39749 4	£3.99
You Have Ghost Mail	Terence Blacker	0 330 39699 4	£3.99
Goodbye, Tommy Blue	Adèle Geras	0 330 41570 0	£3.99
The Ghost of Uncle Arvie	Sharon Creech	0 330 34212 6	£3.99
Olly Spellmaker and the Hairy Horror	Susan Price	0 330 42119 0	£3.99
Olly Spellmaker and the Sulky Smudge	Susan Price	0 330 41582 4	£3.99
Watch Out!	Dina Anastasio and Jane O'Connor	0 330 43415 2	£3.99
Phantom Fun	Jan Burchett and Sara Vogler	0 330 43416 0	£4.99

All Pan Macmillan titles can be ordered from our website, www.panmacmillan.com, or from your local bookshop and are also available by post from:

**Bookpost,
PO Box 29, Douglas, Isle of Man IM99 1BQ**

Credit cards accepted. For details:
Telephone: 01624 677237
Fax: 01624 670923
Email: bookshop@enterprise.net
www.bookpost.co.uk

Free postage and packing in the United Kingdom